Forever Into The Sunset

By

Rebecca Missey

CreateSpace
4900 LaCross Road
North Charleston, SC. 29406

Chapter One

They were inseparable. Charlie was always closer to Corey than a shadow. They were separated by only 18 months, true Irish twins. If you saw them you would not even think they could be brothers. Corey had their mothers baby fine blonde hair, and deep blue eyes. Charlie was all their father with wavy dark hair and gray eyes. If you had asked them what they wanted to be when they grew up Corey would have said "I want to be a fireman, Charlie would have said " I want to be Corey."

Most boys Corey's age would get irritated with a sibling like Charlie. He was always two heartbeats behind him trying to be like him in every way. Not Corey, he loved it. He took his role as oldest sibling very seriously. Life wasn't always easy for Corey and Charlie Miller. Daddy was drunk all of the time. And mama, well mama was what grown ups called manic. All the boys knew was some days she was really happy, and others she was really sad. It seemed to to Corey and Charlie as though there were more sad days than happy. All she did was lay in bed the entire day.

Jake and Betty Miller were married at sixteen. Seven months before Corey was born. Town gossip held that they were second cousins. Small town gossip being what it is, there tends to be at least a shred of truth. Truth, in this case was a bit worse. The truth of it was Jake and Betty were first cousin, once removed. It was a truth Betty fought in vain to keep from her sons.

Most of the time Betty slept. She wanted to die. She prayed for death everyday. On more than one occasion she had tried to take her life. This painfully small life was never something she had wanted. She had never cared for Jake, never mind loving him. Thanks to one night in the barn, full of beer and teenaged curiosity, they were stuck with each other. The truly sad thing was she didn't care how her unhappiness made Corey and Charlie unhappy. At her lowest moments she didn't care at all.

They lived on a pig farm that had been in the family for several generations. They lived in a small two bedroom cabin, there was two hundred acres and a lake. They gave a bad name to the term dirt poor. Corey wanted desperately to escape. "Look what I found." He said holding a five dollar bill in front of Charlie. Charlie, who had been sitting under a shade tree jumped to his feet.

"Where did you find that?"

"Who cares? I am going to buy a guitar with it."

"You stole it from him didn't you?"

"All we do around here I think I earned it. Besides he will never be sober enough to realize its gone. Don't you want better than this Charlie? Everyone says your voice should be on the radio. You and me, we could be the next Everly Brothers, or something."

"Don and Phil Everly aren't permanently caked in pig shit."

"So you are just going to stay here all of your life? Come on Charlie! Come into town with me, help me pick out my guitar."

They practiced every spare minute they could find. They found a couple of other boys to join them, and soon they had a band going. They were playing clubs around the area. By a miracle They had kept it all from Jake and Betty. One afternoon after school the boys entered the house to find Jake sitting at the table with Corey's guitar across his lap. "What is this boys?"

"Its my guitar, daddy."

"I can see that." Jake said as he slammed the guitar

into the tabletop. As he did one of the strings flew off and nearly hit Jake in the face.

"Don't daddy, please. You will ruin it."

"Don't tell me what to do in my house." Jake said as he stood up, knocking the chair over behind him. "You brought this instrument of evil into my house? Answer me boy!" Jake said as he slammed the guitar into the table again, this time cracking the body of it.

"Daddy please, it's mine."

"It's mine if it's in my house." He said as he swung the guitar in the direction of Corey's head. Corey ducked just in time. The guitar hit the kitchen counter instead. Jake flew into a rage then. He rapidly slammed the guitar against the counter. "Devil worship. Devil music. You have damned us all to hell by bringing this shit into my house. God damn you. God damn you both. God damn you. God damn you. God damn you!" The boys ran from the cabin, only stopping once they got to the lake. They both plopped down on the ground.

"I hate this Charlie. I hate it. I wish they would both die. Why can't they both just drop dead?"

" I am sorry Corey. We can get another guitar. We will hide the next one at Billy's house"

"I almost forgot to tell you, I got us a gig in a club in Chicago next weekend. Pointless now I guess."

"Chicago? Corey we have to go."

"Without a guitar? How are we going to go without a guitar?"

"We have to find a way, its a once in a lifetime opportunity. Come on lets go get the guys together and figure this thing out." As it turned out, on of the boys knew someone with a guitar, and they were soon on their way to Chicago.

She was in the front row. She was beautiful, but

somehow she was different than other girls who came out to hear them play. She sang along with every song they played, word for word. Her eyes never left his, or his hers. Charlie had never been more happy to end a gig. He literally jumped off the stage and ran to her. "Hi, I'm Charlie Miler."

"Charlotte Webster."

"Would you like to go get a soda or something?"

""I'd like that."

"Hey Charlie, we have to get back to the bus station." Corey yelled over to his brother from a few feet away.

"Corey I know. I will be back in time." He turned to Charlotte, "Sorry about that my brother needs to learn to worry less. So, where do you want to go?"

"There is a cafe right across the street." At that they left, and went to the cafe and sat down in a both. "How long have you and you brother been playing music?"

9

"We have sang in the church all of our lives, but in clubs its only been a few months. Our parents don't even know we are in a band."

"You mean they don't know you are here? Where do they think you are?"

"They think we are at a friends house."

"That's kinda like me. My friends talked me into coming here tonight. My parents think we are studying for a test. My dad is a preacher, he thinks rock and roll music is-"

"The devils work,yeah mine thinks that way too."

"What does your dad do?"

"He is a farmer." Just then Corey walked though the door.

"Charlie if we don't leave now, we are going to miss the bus." Charlie and Charlotte both stood, he held her hands in his.

"Charlie, will I see you again?"

"Can you meet me here tomorrow afternoon?" She nodded yes. He kissed her on the cheek, followed Corey out of the cafe. Together they walked to the bus stop.

"What the hell was that? You can't meet her tomorrow." They boarded the bus and found a seat at the back.

"I have to Corey."

"What do you mean you have to? What if daddy finds out?"

"I don't care. Charlotte is the girl I am going to marry."

"What the shit Charlie! You just met her. She is far from the slutty girls who usually throw themselves at you when we play. And you have sure as hell never said anything about marriage before."

"This is the girl I am going to marry. I am going to

see her tomorrow."

"Daddy is going to kill you."

"We are not kids anymore Corey. Listen I have been thinking. I am nearly 16, you almost 18. I have saved all of the money we have been making."

"Yeah, me too."

"So, why don't we get our own place?"

"I don't know mama would be there with daddy all on her own."

"So what are you going to do? Stay there and serve as a buffer for the rest of their lives? Think about it okay?"

Charlie went to see Charlotte the next day and soon they were meeting every day. On a typical day they went for a walk in the park. "I want you to meet my mom and dad. Will you join us tomorrow night for dinner? Mom is an excellent cook."

"Are you sure? I can't see a preacher wanting a smelly

pig farmer in his house."

"Don't be silly. Sooner or later we have to meet each others families. I want them to love you too."

"Love, hey?"

"Yes love. Don't you love me?"

"I have loved you from the second I saw you."

"Love at first sight? Maybe you should write a song about that."

"Maybe I will. Actually there is something I wanted to ask you." He said as he took her hand in his and dropped to one knee.

"Oh God Charlie. Oh God."

"Charlotte, I know we have only known each other a few weeks and we are still young, but I know I love you. If you will have me I would be honored if you would marry me." He took a ring box out of his pocket. He opened it and offered it to her. She was trembling, with tears streaming from her eyes.

"Oh Charlie, yes. Yes." He stood, and slipped the ring on her finger. He took her into his arms. They both cried. "Come on I want to tell my parents right away"

"Maybe you should go and talk to your parents by yourself first. Maybe break the ice a little? And we will stick to the plan of me joining you all for dinner tomorrow?"

Chapter 2

"Absolutely not! You are only 17 years old. You are going to finish high school. You are doing to college, if you wish. And then, you will marry someone-" He paused for a second searching for the right word. "Someone suitable."

"Who would be suitable dad? Haven't you always taught me not to judge? What would your congregation think of you not wanting me to marry someone who happens to be a farmers son? You haven't even met him yet."

"That is not my reason for not wanting you to marry now. You are not ready. If you love him now, you will still love him in a few years. Unless, there is something else. Something you have not told us? Is there a baby?"

"No dad."

"Then you will wait. There will be no further discussion on this matter."

"Dad this is not your choose to make."

"Charlotte if you marry this boy or any other before you graduate from college, you will be choosing him over us. It is this boy or us. Charlotte you're education has to come first that is that. Now please go and help your mother clear the table. You and I will go tomorrow to return his ring to him." Charlotte left her fathers den and quietly slipped out of the house. Twenty minutes later

15

she was knocking on Corey and Charlie's apartment door.

"I hope its not too late. I had to see you." Charlie noticed right away that her eyes were red from crying.

"Come in. Of course it isn't too late." They went in and sat down on the sofa. "What's wrong?"

"Dad says we have to wait until I graduate college to get married."

"So we wait. I'm okay with waiting. Maybe he is right. There isn't any rush."

"Charlie I don't want to wait" She reached out and took his hand. She looked deeply into his eyes. "I want to be with you." She leaned in and kissed him gently, first on the month, then slowly with sweet urgency along his neck. He pulled away.

"We don't have to do anything you're not ready for." In response she straddled his lap and began unbuttoning his shirt. They stood, he led her to his room. The early morning sun caressed their naked intertwined bodies as they lie in Charlie's bed. She woke first. She ran her fingers though his hair and kissed his ear. He woke and brushed a stray hair from her face. "Run away with me Charlie. Let's jump on a bus, cross the state line and get married." Without much more thought, they did just that. By noon they were Mr. and Mrs. Charlie Miller.

They fell into an easy routine. Charlotte went to school during the day, while the band rehearsed. Most nights they played in area bars. It wasn't much, but in its simplicity it felt like a fairy tale.

Both Charlie and Charlotte's parents had cut all ties with them. Charlotte's because Charlie was not good enough for their baby girl, and Charlie's because they were ashamed that they would never be good enough. Charlotte and Charlie were too young and in love to care. By the time Charlotte's high school graduation rolled around the band had lined up a regional tour. Life was falling into place.

"Come with us."

"Crammed in a van full of musical equipment with you and four other guys? I think I will pass. Besides, this job is really important to me."

"You're just stuffing advertisements into the newspaper."

"Stuffing circulars in the newspaper today, writing the feature someday. You are following your dream. I need to follow mine."

"I'll be gone for three months. Longer if things go well."

"Then we should make the most of the time we have." Charlotte led Charlie to their bed room.

They band members took turns driving from one gig to

the next. Charlie was the least drunk of the five of them, so tonight was his turn. There was something on he road ahead. By the time Charlie realized it was a large deer, it was too late. The deer came through the windshield. Charlie lost control of the van. The van flipped several times and rolled down an embankment, Metal and glass flew all about. Another car a minute or two back stopped. The driver got out and ran toward the van. When he opened the door he was shocked by what he saw. He tried to hide how sickened he was by what he saw, but he was sure it was all over his face. "Young man, there is a gas station a mile from here. I am going for help. I will be right back." The man ran back to his car. He threw up all over his shoes. Words could not describe what he had seen. In his forty years as an emergency room doctor he had never seen anything more gruesome.

Charlie came out of it without so much as a scratch.

The others were all gone, killed instantly. A piece of glass had been rammed through Corey's heart. Charlie wondered how he would live with killing his brother and three close friends? How would he face their families? His family? How would he tell his mother that Corey was gone?

Chapter 3

It turned out Charlie was right to worry that his mother wouldn't take the news well. Two days after Corey died Betty took on of Jake's guns, put it to her head and pulled the trigger. She simply could not go on without her Corey. Chalie's drinking had steadily gotten worse. He also began using drugs. He told Charlotte he had it all under control. She was afraid for him. She was afraid for them. "I can't do this on my own Charlie. What I make at the paper isn't nearly enough. I know this has all been difficult on you. First Corey then your mom, but we can't go on like this. Charlie I need you to help me."

"Maybe you should go home to your parents. Maybe everyone was right. We were too young to make this work."

"So you are just giving up? After a year?"

"After the year we have had would anyone blame us?"

"That's just it though. When things get a little tough you don't give up, you hold your ground. You're drinking and using way too much,"

"If I am such a mess why do you want this to work?"

"I love you. And its not- Its not just you and I anymore. There will be a baby soon." Her words trailed off and broke up as she spoke. She was scared to death of what his response would be. At first he didn't say anything, as a million thoughts ran through his head.

"What are we going to do?" She reached and took the

beer can from his hand, and sat it down on the table.

"For starters you are going to sober up take a shower and go out and find a job. We are going to take this one step at a time." He didn't find a job. Days soon became weeks. A time or two he did find a job, but he always managed to loss it a day or two later. Charlotte was starting to worry. She said as much to Charlie. "Maybe your dad would have some work for you."

"God Charlotte you can't expect me to go crawling back to him"

"I don't know Charlie. What other choice do we have? It doesn't have to be forever, just until something else comes along."

The next morning Charlie went to see Jake. He found him sitting on the porch of the cabin. "Daddy I need to talk to you about something. Daddy I need work. I was thinking I might come work here on the farm for a while."

"My son is dead, Other so killed him. No son left to come and work on this farm."

"Daddy please. I need work. We are having a baby and I can't-"

"You got that prissy little thing knocked up?"

"Daddy you are not going to be hateful to her."

"You know your mama always wanted a grandchild. If you hadn't killed Corey she wouldn't have killed herself. She'd be here to see this child of yours."

"I didn't kill Corey. And you know damn well Corey and I spent our entire childhoods watching her try over and over again to kill herself. That is all on you."

"You going to live here too?"

"No sir. I will never do that again."

"Be here at five in the morning. Not a second later."

Chapter 4

Jake worked Charlie like an animal. Usually 14 hours a day, always six days a week. Somewhere along the way Charlie and Charlotte decided it would be easier to move to the farm. The baby was born six months after Charlie went to work for his father. It was a girl. They named her Harper.

Early on Charlie talked about getting another band together. His father required him to work such long hours he was drained of all ambition and energy. After a short time he gave up. Charlotte soon gave up her dreams of writing as well. Their forgotten dreams led them to resentment. Charlotte's resentment ate her from the inside. Somewhere along the way,Charlie's drinking and drug use had seduced Charlotte. It pulled her in. It felt so incredible to be able to escape for awhile. Sometimes Harper would be crying and Charlotte would not bring herself to go to her. She was too lost on a cloud of sheer happy, she never wanted to land. One morning Charlotte woke with a blinding pain in her lower belly. "Charlie wake up something is wrong." They stared for the emergency room. The pains were every few minutes.

"Mrs. Miller you are in labor. You are having a baby."

"Baby. No. That's not right. That can't be."

"Yes mam I would say you are about seven months."

"Seven months? No. That can't be. Charlie I don't understand. What are they talking about?"

"This baby will be here any minute. Mrs Miller you need to settle down."

"Settle down? How? How am I supposed to settle down? You are telling me I am seven months pregnant and I didn't even know? I haven't taken care of myself" She was screaming hysterically.

"Mr. Miller with your permission I am going to sedate

your wife we have to deliver this baby, now."

"Yes sir do whatever you have to do," The baby never took a breath.   They named him William Corey. In spite of being born lifeless, William Corey changed all of their lives. The second Charlotte came to in the hospital and realized what had happened, she swore off all drugs and alcohol. A few days later she made a second, and perhaps more important decision.

" I am leaving you Charlie." He didn't respond. "Did you hear me Charlie? I am taking Harper and we are leaving. I need to know you are hearing me."

"You won't leave me. You both love me."

"Harper has never known you sober. When we first met you told me you would never become your father. This shit you are sitting here doing right now is ten times worse than Jake's drinking problem ever could have been. We buried a son because of the way we are living."

"You don't know anything Charlotte. He hit us. Have I ever raised a hand to you or Harper?"

"Am I supposed to stay until things get to that point? Look that girl is almost three years old she has more or less raised herself to this point. That stops tonight. That poor little thing needs to know a normal life."

"Its raining. Wait until morning."

"So what? So you can change my mind? No. I am a big girl I can drive in the rain. She is asleep in the car-"

"You were going to leave without letting me say goodbye?"

"You sober yourself up and you can come and see her. I don't want to keep you two apart. But I won't have her growing up like this." She walked out of the cabin. He followed her. She drove away. Into the rain. Into the dark.

He was passed out on the floor when the phone rang.

For a split second he couldn't figure out where he was or what the noise was. Finally it hit him; the phone was ringing. He rubbed his eyes, got up and fumbled his way across the room. "Hello?"

"Mr Miller. This is Pam Smith with county hospital, You need to get here as soon as you can."

"Why? Has something happened? Has something happened to my wife and daughter?"

"Mr Miller you need to get here as soon as you can." Twenty minutes later Charlie walked into the hospital. He walked to the nurses desk.

"I am Charlie Miler. I got a phone call about my wife and daughter"

"Yes Mr. Miller. There was an accident tonight. Your daughter is in serious but stable condition. In a few days she should be good as new. Would you like to go see her?"

"What about my wife? She would have been driving the car."

"Mr. Miller, why don't we sit down?"

"I don't want to sit down. I want to know how my wife is."

"Mr. Miller there is no easy way to say this. Your wife and daughter were struck head on by the other car. Your wife was killed instantly. I am so sorry." And so to Charlie at least, it seemed as though he was responsible for yet someone else he loved being gone.

Chapter 5

Days passed without Harper and Charlie speaking. Although she was barely three years old, she was almost completely self sufficient. She had to be. Even though Charlie was there in body Harper was alone. Before mommy went away she had once showed Harper how to use the hand held can opener. So, Harper would go to the pantry and get a can of green beans, or whatever open the can and eat it. A time or two a week she would bathe. Every night she would say a prayer and crawl into bed. She always prayed for the same things. She prayed for daddy to pay attention to her. She prayed he would warm up her food. She wasn't sure, but she thought her tummy made funny noises because she always ate everything cold. Most of all, she prayed for mommy to come home from wherever she had gone.

Somewhere along the way Charlie moved his friend Less in with them. Less had owned one of the bars Charlie's band used to play in. Less and Charlie shared similar taste in music and drugs. If it could be injected or smoked Charlie and Less spent all day everyday lying around the living room injecting or smoking it.

Harper was trilled when Less moved in because with him he brought his daughter Jess. Jess and Harper were about the same age and fast friends. They played from sunrise to sundown. They ran all over the property. They made mud pies. They caught butterflies. They played dress up and played with dolls. It didn't matter to each of them what they did as long as they were always together. They knew they would always be friends and nothing would ever pull them apart.

Chapter 6

Time passed as time often does. Jess and Harper were fifteen years old. Less couldn't help but notice how beautiful Harper was becoming. Sometimes the girls would splash around in the lake. Less would sit nearby mesmerized at how sexy Harper's quickly maturing body looked underneath her wet clingy t-shirt. Violent passion pumped through his entire body as he imagined how it would feel to rip that t-shirt from her body.

Harper had a boyfriend, Trevor. Trevor was a real piece

of work. Less had seen him hit Harper more than once.

She needed a protector. She needed a man. She needed

Less.   Trevor and Harper had gotten into another fight,

Less saw her sitting on the porch by herself. She was

holding a bag of frozen peas against her right eye. He got

two beers out of the refrigerator and went to the porch.

He sat down next to her.   He opened one and handed it to

her. She took it. He opened his. "That's one hell of a

shiner you've got there."

"It's nothing. Trevor gets angry sometimes"

"Real men don't hit their ladies." As he spoke her

leaned in and kissed her neck. She jumped up.

"What the hell. I have known you since I was three

years old."

"You're not three anymore." He kissed her again, on

the mouth this time. She didn't stop him. She kissed him

back. She took his hand and led him to her bedroom.

They walked right past Charlie, who was passed out on the floor. Harper shut and locked the door. They swiftly became one, Harper's Thursday "Days of The Week Panties" around her ankles.

After that first time Harper and Less had sex on a regular basis. He gave her money every time. She loved having money. She loved being able to buy new shoes and clothes. The girls at school could no longer make fun of her for wearing out dated patched up ratty clothes. She wondered sometimes if she could find more men who would give her money for sex, but she was afraid that might make her a prostitute. She decided as long as she limited herself to Less she would be okay. Charlie was still completely clueless to what was going on, but Jess was not.

" I know you are sleeping with my dad. You know that's not right."

"Lighten up Jess. No body is getting hurt. It is just sex."

"No one is getting hurt? I'm hurt. Not to mention grossed out. My best friend and my dad?"

"Don't think about it is it bothers you. We can find you your own sugar daddy then you won't be so up tight about it anymore."

"I don't think we can be friends anymore if this continues."

"What is that some kind of an ultimatum? I am not going to stop sleeping with your father. What other part time job pays what he does?"

"That's nasty Harper."

"Hey one girls nasty is another girls ticket to something better. I can't

live here like this forever. I got a bit saved up. Jess you're smart. You will win scholarships you can go to college, I have to find a more creative way."

"So what? Your going to turn tricks all of your life?"

"Less is not a trick. He is my boyfriend. He gives me things."

"He gives you money. That makes you his whore." Harper slapped Jess across the face.

"You're right. This friendship is over. How will we avoid each other in this tiny little cabin?"

"Don't worry about it. I am going to live with my mom's parents."

"Good. Go live with old people you will fit right in." Three days later Jess was on her way to her grandparents. Harper had lost the only friend she had ever had.

Chapter 7

"Are you feeling okay this morning Harper? You don't look so hot."

"Wow dad. You have never shown me any concern.

Maybe you're the one who is sick." She didn't want to admit it but for once Charlie was right. Her stomach had felt weird for a while. She convinced herself it was the flu. There was always something going around school. Charlie, Less and Harper were all sitting around the kitchen table. She had cooked eggs and bacon for them. Twice while she was cooking she had ran off to the bathroom and gotten sick. Days passed she didn't get better. She worked really hard to push the thought out of her head that it could be morning sickness. She and Les had never been even remotely careful. She had no earthly idea when her last period had been. She had no reason to pay any attention to it. God. What if she were pregnant? The thought itself made her sick. She wanted more than this. She wanted to get as far away from the farm and its lifestyle as she could.

After several weeks of feeling like crap she knew she

had to find out on way or the other. So after school on a Tuesday she walked to the drugstore. Her original plan was to wear dark glasses and a baseball cap, but she decided that would end up looking more conspicuous than ever. So she took a deep breath and walked into the store. She felt as though everyone in the store was watching her as she made her way to the "family planning" aisle and grabbed the home pregnancy test. She quickly walked to the counter. "Its for a friend." She said as she laid the box down.

"Yeas dear. It always is." The cashier said as she put the box in a bag and handed it to Harper.

Harper suspected the five minutes she spent waiting for the test results were the longest five minutes in the history of the world. Her mind raced with a million thoughts. How would she finish school? She hated school but she knew she needed to finish. What would

Charlie say? What would Less do? What were the kids at school going to say? She knew she wasn't the only pregnant girl at school, but she was the only one pregnant by someone their parents age. Gross That's what they would say. "Gross little freak." She found it ironic that before she started sleeping with Less she was an outcast. Now, thanks to Less's money she was wearing all the cool clothes and she had fallen in with the cool kids. Now that she was having Less's baby she would be the biggest freak ever. Finally the timer sounded. She looked at the test. It was positive. It wasn't true. She wouldn't allow it to be.

Most days she simply refused to believe it. Maybe the test had been wrong. Aside from throwing up from time to time she hadn't noticed any real difference. Mind over matter. She didn't want a baby, therefore there was not a baby. When someone would say something to her about being sick she quickly dismissed it. She would say something like "Oh I must have picked up a bug at school," or "I have been studying a lot. I am under a lot of stress." It wasn't long though before there were other changes. Her clothes were getting snug.

"Babe are you gaining weight? Don't go losing that beautiful little figure on me now." Less said as he put his arm around her waste and pulled her in close. Harper pulled away.

"Don't call me babe. I don't want to do this anymore."

"You don't want to do what anymore?"

"This. Us. Whatever we are its done."

"What? You don't love me anymore?"

" I never loved you."

"You love the money I give you. You love all the pretty things my money buys you. You love the way I make you feel." Harper backed away from Less.

"It's done Less"

"Nothing is done unless I say it is." He grabbed her arm and pulled her into a kiss. She tried to push him away. He held tight to her arm.

"Less please don't be rough with me. You'll hurt the baby." Less let go of Harper's arm. All of the color drained away from his face.

"What baby?"

"Our baby. I am pregnant."

"Shit. Do you want me to drive you to the abortion clinic?"

"What a heartless thing to say. No I don't want you to drive me anywhere. I am going to tell Charlie everything."

"Tell him what a dirty little girl you have been with Uncle Less. He won't believe you. Now listen here. We are going to end this pregnancy, and we are going to continue on just as we have been. And from now on you will be more careful. There will be no more baby scares."

"I am telling my daddy."

"Harper I am telling you he will not believe you. When has he ever been a father to you?"

"You had better hope you're right." She said as she rushed off to find Charlie. She knew Less was right, but she didn't know what else to do. One way or the other the situation had to change. How could it get any worse? Harper knew just where to find Charlie. She found him sitting at the lake. "Daddy do you have minute?" Harper said as she sat down in the chair beside him. As Harper sat down Less stormed up behind them.

"Its a lie Charlie. Whatever she has told you it is all lies."

"I haven't told him anything yet Less. Why don't you

pull up a chair. Maybe you would like to tell him?"

"Would one of you just tell me."

"Less and I have been having sex for about four months now. He pays me for it. I am having his baby."

"It's a lie Charlie."

"Less I know it's a lie. Harper that is disgusting how could you even think of saying such a thing? Less would never cross that line. He has been like family to you and I for all of these years."

"Where do you think I have been getting money to buy all of the new clothes I have?"

"Harper I really don't want to hear this. Less would never do something so low."

"How can you believe him over me?"

"Because he is telling the truth. You are saying evil, vile, harmful things." Harper ran to the cabin. She closed and locked her bedroom door. She flung herself onto the bed. Tears burst forward. She cried like she had never cried before. Sixteen years of pain and anguish spilled onto her pillow. "Mama, Mama what am I supposed to do?" From her open bedroom window she could here Charlie and Less talking and laughing. What Harper had told her father had meant nothing to him. To Charlie it would seem, water was thicker than blood. She cried until she ran herself completely out of tears and energy. She drifted off to sleep.

Chapter 8

Harper woke before dawn. She threw a few belonging into a bag. She slipped out of the cabin. She hitchhiked to the nearest bus station. By the time she got there a plan had formed. She had never met her mothers parents, or if she had she must have been to young to remember all she had of them was their address on an envelope she had held onto all of these years. She figured they were her only hope.

Two days later she arrived at the house her mother had grown up in. As she stood in the driveway she couldn't believe what she was seeing. "Good God mama why did you ever leave this?" She had never seen anything like the house in front of her. It looked like something from one of those house and garden magazines. Harper didn't know anything about house designs but it reminded her of "Gone With The Wind." There were flower beds everywhere. Off in the distance she noticed a pool and horse stable. "I guess if a girl has to run away this is the kind of place to go." Hesitantly Harper rang the doorbell. A few seconds later a regal woman in her mid sixties answered the door.

"May I help you?"

"I hope so."

"Whatever you are selling we don't need it." She

started to close the door.

"Mam please wait. I am Charlotte's daughter."

"Harper? Is that no count father of yours here? Has he put you up to asking us for something?"

"No mam. I am here by myself."

"Well you should have called. Come in. I was just getting ready to have a cup of tea. Would you care for a cup?" Without waiting for an answer she poured two cups. She gave Harper one. They sat opposite each other in the living room. "So child what brings you here? I have never seen so much as a picture of you. Now here you are out of the clear blue?"

"Forgive me. I am sorry for just turning up like this. I didn't know where else to go." Harper told her grandmother the entire story of her and Less and how Charlie had not believed her.

"You were right in coming here. We will figure this

all out. First thing first." She stood and picked up both of their teacups. "You have traveled for a couple of days?"

"Yes mam."

"We need to get you into a shower." She led her upstairs. "This will be your bedroom while you are here. It was your mothers room when she was growing up. There is an adjoining bathroom. It is your private bathroom. The closet is stocked with shampoo, soap and towels. Help yourself. If you find you need something that the room is not stocked with please let me know. If you need anything your grandfather and I will be downstairs. Enjoy your shower and have a nap if you like. Dinner will be ready in about an hour." Katherine walked out of the room. She went downstairs. She entered her husbands den, He was at his desk as she knew he would be. "Harold you will never believe who is upstairs."

"Jesus."

"Better."

"Better than our lord and savior?"

"Harper, our granddaughter."

"Our granddaughter? Upstairs? Her low life father is with her I assume." He took his glasses off and put them aside.

"No. She ran away from him. She needs our help rather desperately. She is staying as long as she wants."

"How do we know this girl is who she says she is? She could be running some sort of a scam."

"Harold don't be foolish. She looks exactly like Charlotte at that age. We made horrible mistakes with Charlotte. If we had done better by her she might still be alive. I pray everyday for a way to hurt less for the way we treated Charlotte."

"No matter what we do to help this child Charlotte will never come back."

"I know that Harold." Katherine took a deep breath and told Harold everything Harper had told her.

"Good God. Should we help Harper file statutory rape charges?"

"No. I think the poor thing has been though more than enough."

"She should have been living here all along."

"Well, be that as it may, it doe little good to dwell on the past. All we can do is help her now."

"What will we do?"

"Get her enrolled in a good school. Help her find a good home for her baby."

"You know come to think of it Mr. and Mrs Clarke came to me a few days ago. They asked me to encourage the congregation to pray for God to send them a baby."

"Oh Harold! That's marvelous. They are a perfect couple. Isn't simply amazing how the Lord works?"

"Yes my dear it certainly is. Shall we bring this issue up with Harper this evening?"

"Perhaps we should let her get settled in first."

"You might be right. So when do I get to meet her?"

"She will be done for dinner shortly."

The dinning room felt overwhelmingly formal to Harper. There were candles and flowers in the center of the table. Eight chairs sat around it. Suddenly she felt like a fish out of water. Katherine was sitting at one end. Harold was at the other end. There was a place in between them for Harper. Harper approached the table. "Darling this is your granddaughter. Harper, this is your grandfather, Harold."

"Harper how good it is to meet you. Please have a seat." Harper sat down.

"Did you have a nice rest dear." Katherine said as she scooped a serving of roast from the platter and passed it to Harper.

"Yes mam. Thank you" Harper helped herself and passed it on to Harold.

"Do you think you will be comfortable here?" Harold asked as he took the platter from her.

"Yes sir. It is not what I am used to but I think I will adjust." They finished their meal. They did their best to get to know each other. After dinner Harper returned upstairs. It had been a long day and she was eager to get a good nights sleep. Harold and Katherine remained in the living room.

"Poor girl. Do you think she will go for our plan?"

"I surely hope so. I will introduce her to Leonard and Claire tomorrow when I enroll her at school. We will take it from there."

Leonard and Claire Clarke had known each other all of their lives. Well, almost. They had met on the first day of kindergarten. Neither of them had thought for a second of loving anyone else. They officially started dating sophomore year of high school. Never for a second had their love faltered. For Claire and Leonard there simply was not anyone else. Now they both worked at the school they had attended. Claire was a second grade teacher and Leonard was the school counselor. They were married a week after college graduation. Claire taught during the day and waited tables in the evenings while Leonard pursued his Master and his PhD. They wanted to start a family right away. Claire became pregnant right away. She miscarried at six weeks. As high as the happiness had taken them the despair had pulled them done equally as far. They suffered three more miscarriages before consulting a fertility specialist. Their worst fears were confirmed. They would never have children of their own. They were heartbroken. After a while they decided to explore adoption. Claire had her heart set on a newborn. She knew she would love any child but her very soul craved a baby, so they put their names on the waiting list and started the process. When Katherine approached them with their granddaughter's story it all seemed too good to be true.

"I don't want to get our hopes up and lose another baby."

"Claire there is always a chance of losing the baby no matter what route we take. Birth parents back out at the last minute all of the time. God has sent us this young lady. We have to trust in his plan no matter what it is. There is nothing lost by meeting with her." They sat up a meeting with Harper for Friday afternoon.

Chapter 9

Harper loved the freedom of driving. The weather was spectacular. The temperature was 75. There wasn't a cloud in sight. She turned the radio up and opened the windows. She felt free and happier than she had been in a long time. She lost track of how fast she was going. That is, until she saw the blue and red lights behind her. "Shit." She pulled over. The policeman approached the car.

"Do you know why I pulled you over?" He was beautiful. She knew boys were not beautiful. Beautiful was not what she meant. No way did handsome even come close to doing him justice. He was beautiful. Beautiful like lying naked on a beach in June. This she knew would be the love of her life.

"Yes sir. I know I was speeding. I am truly sorry."

"Where were you off to in such a hurry?"

"Would you believe the library?"

"The library? That's a first."

"I'm meeting Mr. and Mrs. Clarke."

""They're good folks. Claire was my second grade teacher."

"Does everyone around here know everyone else or what?"

"Pretty much. You're not from here?"

"No. I am staying with my grandparents."

"The preacher and his wife. I was pretty sure this was their car when I pulled you over. I am supposed to write you a ticket."

"Oh yeah?"

"I was thinking I might forget to write the ticket if you agree to go to dinner with me."

"What are you doing? Running some sort of a scam

pulling young women over to ask them out?"

"I swear I've never done that before."

"Throw in not telling Harold and Katherine and you've got yourself a deal."

"I will pick you up at seven, that is if you will be back from the library by then."

"Seven sounds good."

"Okay. You drive safe now." He went back to the patrol car and drove off. Harper drove the rest of the way to the library thinking about this boy she barely knew and how she knew she was already falling in love with him.

As she walked into the library Claire and Leonard waved at her from a table in the back "Hello Harper. It is good to see you again. This is my husband Leonard. Leonard this is Harper. Harper have a seat." Harper sat down.

"Harper it is nice to meet you. My wife tells me you

are having a baby."

"Yes that is true."

"Claire and I wish to offer a solution."

"Not that your baby is a problem."

"No. No not at all. But at your age we thought maybe you would like to pursue other goals. I'm not saying a child would prevent you from accomplishing your goals, but one could surely slow you down. You may want to go to college or travel. You will have plenty of time for children later. Not that we are trying to talk you out of your baby. What you do is your choice."

"Yes, naturally it is your choice. What my husband is trying to say is we have tried for may years to have a baby. We would be honored if you would allow us to adopt this baby. We would give this baby a good life. Your baby would grow up in a two parent home. As you know we both work at the school. We are well established in our careers. And, if you like you could remain a part of the child's life. We would sit down with or lawyer and figure it all out."

"As I told my grandmother yesterday I am going to want some time to think this all though."

"Of course. Take all the time you need." As Leonard spoke they all three stood. They said their goodbyes and went their separate ways.

He rang the doorbell at exactly seven. He was dressed in slacks and a blazer. He held a single red rose. Harold answered the door. "Bradley. Good evening. It is nice to see you. Come in. Harper will be right down. Please have a seat. Would you like something to drink."

"No sir." Bradley sat down. Harold poured himself a drink and sat down opposite Bradley.

"Bradley, Harper is only sixteen. You're what now twenty-two? That is a sizable age difference. Especially at her age. I am allowing her to go out with you because I have known you all of your life. I have known both of your parents most of theirs. I know you are a good young man. Don't prove me wrong."

"Yes sir. I know what you mean." Katherine and Harper joined them. Harper looked perfect in a simple black dress. Bradley handed her the rose. "This is for you. You look beautiful."

"Thank you."

"I will put the rose in a vase in your room."

"Thank you Katherine." She handed the rose to Katherine. She took Bradley's hand.

Harper couldn't help but feel the evening had been magical. They hadn't gone anywhere or done anything special. They had just gone to a movie and dinner. She felt changed by meeting him. She felt as though his soul and hers were one. She couldn't help but think Bradley was the man she was created for. In the days to come they were inseparable. She told him about the baby, about Less, and about her crappy childhood. He wasn't phased by any of it for a second. There truly was one perfect person for everyone. Harper and Bradley knew they had found that someone.

They sat quietly on a park bench. "Harper I have been thinking. Have you signed any papers saying you are giving this baby to the Clarke's?"

"No. Claire is worried she will get too attached to the baby if we do anything official before it is born. After the baby comes we are signing papers. Why?"

"Harper I have been thinking. Claire and Leonard are wonderful people. Any baby would be lucky to have them as parents. And you don't want to be a single parent without a job or anything. Trust me I completely understand that. But there is another choice."

"I already told you Less wanted me to have an abortion, that was a big part of why I left."

"No Harper there's another choice. Harper I have loved you from the start. I love this baby. Harper keep this baby. I will be with you every step of the way." As he spoke he dropped to one knee, and took a ring box out of his pocket. "Harper marry me."

Chapter 10

"She is too young." Harold said as he slammed his morning paper down on the dining room table. Harold and Katherine were sitting at the dining room table. Kathrine had just told Harold about Bradley's proposal"This is exactly what we went through with Charlotte. I knew this would happen."

"Not yet. You don't have to react the way you did with Charlotte."

"I should let her get married at sixteen?"

"She is going to marry him either way. If you forbid it we will lose Harper just as we did Charlotte. Besides Bradley is not Charlie. Bradley is a good young man. He will be a wonderful father and husband. We couldn't have found a better match for her.

"So we give our consent for our sixteen year old granddaughter to get married? What about Claire and Leonard?"

"Yes Harold it will be heartbreaking for Claire and Leonard. But think of how wonderful it will be to have a baby in the family."

"She must finish school do we at least agree on that?"

"Yes Harold I agree."

Everyone agreed that Harper was the most beautiful bride they had ever seen. Harper and Bradley were married in Harold's church on a perfect Saturday in early

June. Harper was quickly approaching her due date. Katherine insisted that Harper hold an oddly large bouquet in all of their pictures. Harper was a little annoyed but she went along with it.

The baby was born two weeks later. They named her Marilyn. Harper was so glad she didn't look anything like Less. She beautiful. Harper loved her so much she was sure her heart would explode. Tears of so much happiness spilled down her face. She had spent so much of her pregnancy thinking of the baby as Claire and Leonard's she had not allowed herself to become attached. Now that her baby was in her arms the love she felt for her was total and complete.

Life fell into a perfect rhythm. Harper knew that she had survived Charlie and Less and come out on the side better than she had ever been. For the first time in her life she was happy. She loved every second of her life now. 2Am feedings or making Bradley a meal when he came home at all hours of the day or night. It suited her and it showed. They bought a small house a few miles from Harold and Katherine. It wasn't much just two bedrooms, but it felt like home. It felt perfect. Katherine took care of Marilyn during the day while Harper finished school. Harold and Katherine encouraged Harper to go to college. She said she would but she wanted to wait until Marilyn stared school. There would be plenty of time for that later. For now she was content being Marilyn's mom and Bradley's wife.   Harper and Bradley both wanted more children, but for that there would also be plenty of time.

Bradley was working the midnight shift. They made love before he left. She lay naked in the moonlight after he left. She couldn't sleep for wanting him so desperately. Surely no one had ever loved anyone the way Harper loved Bradley. She counted the hours until he would return home. Just before day break she drifted off to sleep. The phone rang. "Hello."

"Hello Harper its me, Pete. Will you be around the house for a while this morning?" Pete was Bradley's partner. He had become a good friend to both Bradley and Harper.

"Pete what is it? What's happened to Bradley?"

"Harper just stay put okay? I will be right over." Minutes later Harper and Pete were sitting in her living room. Pete told her what had happened but not a word of it registered. She couldn't make any of it make sense. A fourteen year old kid. A gun. Point blank range. The Seven Eleven on main. Bradley walked in on. In progress. Dead. Dead instantly. "Do you want me to call someone Harper?"

"No. I need to go and check on Marilyn." Pete left

Harper's. His next stop was Harold and Katherine's. As soon as they heard the news they rushed to Harper's. Katherine found Harper and Marilyn in the middle of Marilyn's bedroom floor. Harper was clinging to her child like a life raft. "Young lady your great grandfather is in the kitchen with a brand new box of strawberry ice cream. Would you go and make sure he doesn't eat all of it please." Marilyn hurried from the room. Katherine quickly took Marilyn's place next to Harper in the floor.

"I can't do this Grandma. Not without Bradley."

"Yes you can. You can and you will. You still have Marilyn, me, and your Grandpa. That is not going to change anytime soon. What happened to Bradley was tragic and senseless, but God is here with us. God will get us all through this. Have you told Marilyn yet?"

"No. She knows I am sad but she doesn't know why. How do you tell a four year old child the only man she has ever known as dad is gone?"

"I will handle that. Don't worry about it."

"Oh God. What about the funeral?"

"Your grandfather and I will take care of everything."

"What will I to do now?"

"Cry. Scream. Break something. Pray. All of the above. Do whatever you need to do."

Bradley's funeral was attended by hundreds of people. Entire police departments from towns as far away as six hundred miles away turned up. The outpouring of love and support had been overwhelming. Harper had no clear memories of that day. Everything passed in a blur. Day after day passed much the same way. After the funeral Katherine and Harold demanded that Marilyn and Harper move in with them. It was that Harper was in no shape to look after herself, never mind looking after Marilyn.

She didn't get dressed. She barely got out of bed. She wasn't eating. Her clothes were getting baggy on her. She looked as though she would soon follow Bradley to the grave. Katherine was scared that was exactly what she wanted . She prayed something would happen to pull Harper out of this depression.

Katherine found Harold asleep in his chair. A book open in his lap. She had found him this way hundreds of times over the years. He had never known when to put away what he was working on leave it for another day and go to bed. He had to sit there in that chair until sleep overtook him. "Harold breakfast is on the table. You know you will not eat you're eggs once they are cold." She nudged his arm. "Harold." He didn't respond. She touched his hand. It was cold and clammy. Katherine's stomach flipped over itself and twisted in a million knots. She checked for a pulse. There wasn't one. She held her hand in front of his mouth in search of breath.   There wasn't any. "Harold no! You can't do this to me." She fell to his feet. "I can't breathe without you." Tears quickly stained his suede house slippers.

You here people talk about dying of a broken heart. Katherine did more than talk. She pulled it off. She simply couldn't imagine   how to live without him. She loved him before she had been old enough to know what it meant to love. She admired him. She loved him. She hated him. Yes, at times she had worshiped him. He had been a constant in her life. They had shared a connection like the oceans and the moon. He took her very soul with him to the grave. Without Harold, Katherine was void of a reason to live.   Three months to the day after Harold passed away, Katherine was gone. Losing both her grandparents in such a short time jolted Harper into realizing she had to pull her act together.

Chapter 11

Two days after Katherine's funeral Harper received surprising news. She got a phone call from Harold and Katherine's lawyer. He wanted to see her right away. "Young lady let me start by saying how sorry I am for your recent loss. Your grandparents were both wonderful people. I have some news for you. Their house and all of its contents are now yours." Harper was floored. At first the words didn't make any sense.

"I don't mean to sound ungrateful. This is truly the most amazing thing that has ever happened to me. But could I sell the house? It's thirty five rooms and it's way too much house for just me and my daughter. I would like to sell it and buy the house I am renting."

"You may do what ever you wish."

"Could you handle that for me?"

"I would be happy to. Consider it done." The house

sold quickly. It sold for 1.5 million dollars. Harper was able to purchase the rental house for $65,000. Needless to say she and Marilyn would have enough money to last a while. The thing about money is it brings people out of the woodwork. And when people come out of the woodwork nine times out of ten, they're people you didn't want to deal with again. Harper would learn this the hard way.

It was a hot summer afternoon. Harper was taking groceries out of the trunk of her car. She heard a familiar voice behind her "Harper you sure are looking good." She dropped the bag and spun around.

"Less how did you find us?"

"That's no way to greet an old friend." He reached a brushed a stray hair from her face.

"Don't touch me. Why are you here?"

"I want to see my kid. What did we end up with?"

"I had a daughter. And you will never be a part of her life."

"I have every right to see my daughter. Harper we can keep this between us or we can involve lawyers. That is up to you."

"Why now Less? She is nearly five years old where have you been?"

"I have been trying to pull myself together so I could be a good dad for her."

"When I told you I was pregnant your response was to offer to drive me to the abortion clinic."

"I am a better man now babe."

"She's at a friend's. I need to talk to her about you before she meets you. Stop back by tomorrow morning."

Less started coming to visit nearly everyday. Harper had to admit he was pretty good with Marilyn. Harper loved having help with Marilyn. Harper loved Marilyn more than air, but it was still nice to get away from the house without her from time to time. It was good to be able to go to the grocery store without Marilyn wanting everything she saw. Less and Marilyn were getting along well. It was good for all three of them. On one such afternoon Harper returned home to find Marilyn sitting in the middle of the living floor coloring. "Hey baby. Where is your father?"

"I don't know."

"What do you mean you don't know?" She went though the house calling for him. "Less? Less where are you?" As she entered the kitchen she noticed one of the cabinet doors was ajar. Her heart stopped. It was where she kept important documents. "God please let me be wrong." Harper wasn't wrong. The checkbook was gone. She called the bank. All the inheritance money was gone. Son of bitch left Harper $1.00. Life had once again kicked Harper up side the head.

Harper got drunk that night. And several nights after. Life had knocked her down so many time she failed to see the reason to get back up.

Chapter 12

Ms. Tootsie   had a lot of cats. Truth be told Ms. Tootsie had too may cats. She had so many she had no idea how many she had. It felt like their number changed everyday. Her husband died some ten years ago. The night he passed away a stray cat wondered onto her porch. She couldn't very well turn the poor thing away. She hadn't turned any stray cats away since then. The cats had been Ms. Tootsie's only companionship. That is until a dirty faced runt of a little girl wandered onto her yard one day. "Just what do you think you are doing?"

"Mama says not to talk to strangers."

"Oh I see. So it's all right to come wandering onto my

yard, but not to talk to me?" The child looked

dumfounded. "Never mind. I suppose you're after this."

Ms. Tootsie picked up the child's vibrant purple ball and

tossed it to her. "Child you look like you haven't eaten

in a month of Sundays. Why don't you come on in and I'll

fix you up something to eat?" Marilyn's head told her

this was a bad idea but her tummy overruled her head.

She followed Ms. Tootsie into the house. "You go ahead

and have seat there at the table." There were cats

everywhere. On the table. In the chairs. On the

counters, and even on top of the refrigerator. The smell

of ammonia and uncleanness hung in the air like a veil.

As Marilyn pulled out a chair to sit in a cat jumped out of

it. Marilyn jumped.

"You sure do have a lot of cats."

"God's greatest gift to us is cats. They know when to

curl up in your lap, and they know when to leave you

alone." As she spoke she prepared a grilled cheese sandwich and a bowl of tomato soup. While the food cooked Ms. Tootsie grabbed a wash cloth and washed Marilyn's face. "Now that is much better. I can see your beautiful face now." She put a bowl of soup and sandwich in front of Marilyn. Ms. Tootsie said down across from Marilyn. "Child you and I are long overdue for introductions. Folks around her call me Ms. Tootsie. What do the call you?"

"Marilyn."

"That's not a name you hear very often."

"Mama named me after some movie star."

"Marilyn Monroe."

"Yeah that's it." As Marilyn spoke she began eating as though she was starving.

"Honey when was the last time you ate?"

"I had a candy bar this morning."

"No. I mean real food. Like this," Marilyn held her spoon in mid air, thinking. "Honey if you have to think about it, its been too long. Is your mama sick or something?"

"She sleeps a lot here lately. There are always nasty smelling bottles around her while she's asleep."

"Has something happened lately to upset her?"

"My daddy came to stay with us for a while. I never knew him before. Then one day he was just gone again."

"I see." Ms. Tootsie went to the stove and returned with another grilled cheese. Marilyn finished the second sandwich as quickly as she had the first.

"I probably should be getting home,"

"Well, come back anytime."

For Marilyn Ms. Tootsie's became the place to be. She fed Marilyn's belly. More importantly she fed her mind. She taught her how to break beans fresh from the garden. She taught her how to carefully follow a recipe. She taught her not only how to read, but how to read from the bible. She taught her about Jesus. "Child He is always with us. He sees our every move. His hand is on our shoulders always guiding our every move."

"But I can't see him."

"Honey you don't have to see everything you believe. You believe I love you don't you?"

"Yes mam."

"You can't see my love can you? Jesus is like that."

"Jesus is love?"

"Jesus is love. Jesus is the very reason for getting out of bed in the mornings. Jesus gives us the strength to face this tough old world." Sometimes Ms. Tootsie and Marilyn would just sit on the porch with tall glasses of lemonade. Hours would pass without a word being spoken. There was an easy comfort between them. In a friendship such as this, words were often unnecessary. They had changed each other for the better. Marilyn couldn't imagine life without Ms. Tootsie.

The dark clouds rolled in quickly. Marilyn sat at her desk at the back of the classroom. As usual she was lost in a daydream. The sound of the tornado siren jolted her back to the here and now. As they had practiced a million times, they went out of the classroom and knelt down along the wall. This was not a drill. This was all too real. Marilyn's heart pounded so hard she was sure it would fly out of her chest and get sucked into the tornado. She almost panicked then she remembered Jesus, and everything Ms. Tootsie had taught her. A calm fell over her. Glass and debris blew all around her. She knew she and her classmates would be fine. And they were. Still as school was dismissed she couldn't shake this feeling that something was wrong. She ran from the bus stop as quickly as she could. As she approached Ms. Tootsie's house she could see storm damage to every house on the block. Ms. Tootsie's house was untouched. The knots in her stomach loosened. Marilyn entered the house. "Ms. Tootsie when that siren sounded I was so scared then I remembered what you taught me and-" She walked into the living room and froze in her tracks. Ms. Tootsie was lying on the floor. A heavy Jesus statue lying on the floor next to her head. There was a puddle of blood all around her. Her eyes were wide open, fixed on heaven. Marilyn dropped to her knees. She checked for a pulse. There wasn't one. She listened for a heartbeat. There was none. She breathed for the old woman. No breath was returned. "Ms. Tootsie! No. No!" Anger and sadness mixed together and fell from her eyes as quick, hot tears. She ran from the house and up the road, home.

Her young eyes almost couldn't believe what she saw.

There sat her mother on the ground in front of a pile of bricks and boards where their house had stood that morning. There was nothing left. "I can't do this anymore Marilyn. I can't face shit like this anymore. Why didn't your father take you with him? It would be so much easier if your father had taken you with him."

"Ms. Tootsie is dead."

"There isn't anything I can do about that. Everybody leaves if you don't do the leaving first Marilyn."

"We can't just leave her there." Harper knew Marilyn was right. Together they went back to Ms. Tootsie's house. Harper called 911. And then she called Ms. Tootsie's son. Harper dialed the number. She told him who she was and why she was calling. His response was cold and unfeeling.

"Well, thank you for calling. Have the funeral without me. I can't get away." That was all. He hung up without another word. The funeral was two days later. No one came. Only Harper and Marilyn. As they stood there at the grave site Harper wondered if that would be her someday? Only in her case she worried not even Marilyn would not show up. She knew it was time to start again. The only thing she knew to do was pick up and move again.

Chapter 13

The day after the funeral the humane society came and took all of Ms. Tootsie's cats. A few days after that the city condemned the house. They said the cats caused so much damage it was beyond repair. The city inspector literally came out of the house shaking his head in disbelief. The morning the wrecking ball was rammed into what had been Ms. Tootsie's house Harper and Marilyn left town for good. In her heart Marilyn knew childhood as she knew it had ended. "Where are we going mama?"

"Baby we are going until we stop. Then we will be were we need to be." Harper drove until Marilyn was hungry. Then she would pull of the highway and find a restaurant. She would park close to the dumpster. Sooner or later someone would toss in a part of a sandwich or pizza. She would wait until no one was watching, scurry over to the dumpster and retrieve it.

"Its trash mama."

"It's food Marilyn. It wasn't trash two minutes ago, It will hold you for now." At night they slept in the car along side the road, or at a rest stop if one happened d to be near. Early in the morning on the third day Harper coasted the car into the parking lot of a grocery store just as the car ran out of gas. "We're here Marilyn."

"Where?"

"Where we need to be. You'll see Marilyn. This is

going to work out. Look, look. There is a "help wanted" sign in the window. And look" Harper said as she pointed to a gas station at the far end of the parking lot. "I can run to the gas station change clothes and go into the grocery store and apply for the job. Its all a miracle Marilyn. It's all going to be okay. Now you have to promise me while I am gone you can not so much as move from this spot. Do you hear me?" Harper left the car, her change of clothes in hand. She hurried to the gas station. She found the restroom and changed. Forty five minutes later she returned to the car. Her face was lit up like a Christmas tree. "I got the job." Harper exclaimed as she burst into the car. Mother and daughter both screamed with delight. Marilyn threw her arms around Harper's neck.

"Does this mean no more trash food?' Harper returned her hug and laughed.

"Yes baby girl this means no more trash food." She broke their embrace. "Now we have to find some way to get this car out of the parking lot."

"Look what I found under the seat." Harper couldn't believe her eyes. There, in Marilyn's hand was a folded twenty dollar bill.

"Holly crap. We sure must have a guardian angel with us today. Come on Marilyn. We have a gas can in the back of the car. We will get a bit of gas, a loaf of bread and a jar of peanut butter. That will hold us over for a while." They got out of the car. They walked hand in hand to the gas station. They sang and laughed every step of the way. They got what they needed and paid for it. On the way out the door, a notice on the bulletin board caught Harper's eye. "Boarding House. Good rooms. Great Rates." Harper took the notice off of the bulletin board and walked back to the counter. "Excuse me. This boarding house is this near by?"

"Yes mam. Take a left out of the parking lot, you can't miss it."

It was a two story farm house. It looked as though it could stand a little tlc. Harper figured anything would be better than sleeping in the car. They got out of the car and walked toward the house. An elderly gentlemen stood up from the porch swing and started to hobble toward them. He wore pinstriped pants with suspenders, a white dress shirt and a newsboy hat. He puffed smoke from a pipe. "Can I help you ladies?"

"We are here about the room for rent. Is it still available?"

"Yes it is. Would you like to see it?"

"Well we just arrived in town today. I start work at the grocery store tomorrow and-"

"You want to stay here rent free."

"Only until I get my first paycheck. Please sir my daughter and I need a place to stay."

"Do you cook?"

"I'm sorry?"

"You cook me three meals a day until you get paid."

"Yes sir. That sounds more than fair."

"Come in then I will show you the room." They followed him in and upstairs. The room only had two pieces of furniture. A fourposter bed and an armoire. Both were in a deep cherry finish and looked very old. Harper figured they were likely antique. The room felt tacky. The bedspread was burnt orange with blue flowers. The carpet was well worn and dirty. "Well supper will not fix itself. I expect to be eating in an hour." At that he closed the door behind him and left.

Days rolled on as days tend to do. Work wasn't going

very well. Harper knew she wasn't catching on to how to work the cash registrar as she should. "You have to move more quickly Harper. Do you not see this line you have backed up here?" She heard that all day everyday. Finally on the third day "Harper as always you have fifteen customers backed up. Go ahead and clock out. This isn't working out."

"But Mr. Watson, I can improve I just need to-"

"No Harper. I have already given you longer than I should have."

It was Harper's twenty fifth birthday. She spent it sitting alone in the dark. Drinking. How had she come so far in the wrong direction? Everyday of her life had been made up of layers of mistakes. Maybe that was her purpose in life. To struggle. After all what else had she ever known? "Damn you mama. Why did you leave me?

Why did you have to die? Why couldn't I have gone too?" She drank everything alcoholic drink she could find. She drank until she passed out.

The morning sun burned into her face violently. Harper's head hurt so badly she could not hold it up. She tried to sit up. Just then Marilyn walked into the room. "Marilyn baby,could you get mama a cup of coffee?"

"Okay mama." Marilyn went to the kitchen. "Mama the coffee pot is empty."

"Do you remember how I showed you to make it? Could you make me some?"

"Okay mama." Marilyn knew that the coffee was stored in the cabinet above the stove. She pushed a kitchen chair in front of the stove and climbed into it. Marilyn opened the cabinet and got the can of coffee. As she did the chair gave way beneath her. She screamed as she crashed to the floor.

"Marilyn! Marilyn!" Harper jumped up from the sofa and knelt next to Marilyn's motionless body. "Marilyn dammit you had better be okay." Marilyn groaned and tried to sit. "No baby don't try to get up. I'm going to call the ambulance." Twenty minutes later Harper and Marilyn were in an exam room wailing for the doctor. When the doctor walked into the room Harper couldn't believe her eyes. "Jess? Is that you?" The young woman looked over at Harper. Harper could see the question on her face. Then all at once the light bulb came on.

Chapter 14

"Harper? Good God. Is that you? My God it is good to see you." Jess crossed the room and put her arms around her childhood best friend. Harper returned Jess's hug. Jess broke their embrace and directed her attention to Marilyn. "Climbing in a chair? Young lady that's not very smart."

"No mam." Jess turned to the nurse and ordered test. Then she spoke to Harper.

"Harper could I speak to you outside?" Both ladies stepped outside the door. "How have you been?"

"I'm okay, Look at you! You always said you would be a doctor. I am so proud of you Jess."

"Thanks. Harper I have to ask Marilyn is my half sister isn't she?" Harper nodded in response She proceed to give Jess the condensed version of the past nine years.

"Harper I am sorry. I wish I could tell you were to find Less but I am afraid I haven't heard from my dad since I left all of those years ago."

"Don't worry about it. I am sure Less and the money are long gone. How about you? It looks like you are doing well."

"I am just starting out. I graduated six months ago."

"Still you are doing exactly what you always wanted to do. Jess that is so amazing."

"Thanks. Oh I didn't tell you the best part." She reached for a simple golden chain and pulled it out from under her shirt collar. At the end of the chain was an engagement ring. The band was 14k white gold. The center diamond was ¾ carat round diamond. The rest of the band was covered in smaller, delicate diamonds. Simply put, it was breathtaking.

"Jess it is stunning. Details?"

"He is a few years older than us. He is a surgeon here at the hospital I met him a while back, when I did an internship here. We are getting married next June. Harper you must come. Will you?"

"I would like that."

" I'd love to have more time to reconnect with you and

to get to know Marilyn. Why don't you both come and stay with us? We have plenty of room. I think there s a job open here at the hospital in laundry. I would be happy to put in a good word for you. Everybody wins. I get to know my baby sister and you get a chance to get back on your feet."

"Jess I couldn't ask you for all of that."

"You didn't ask. I offered. Come on lets go check on Marilyn." They walked arm and arm back into Marilyn's room. Harper and Jess both felt as though there friendship had never been lost. Like they stepped back into each others lives without missing a beat.

From the very beginning something about Craig didn't set right with Harper. More than a dozen times she had caught him staring at her. She would pass him in the hallway and he would "accidentally" brush up against her. She would hand him the salt at supper and his hand would always touch hers. She called him out on it every time. He always downplayed it. "I am sorry. It's no big deal is it?"

Harper had the apartment to herself. Or so she thought. It was a hot, sticky summer afternoon. She was wearing a spaghetti strap tank top and a pair of "Daisy Dukes." Craig stood in the doorway, watching her. She was on her hands and knees picking Marilyn's toys up off the floor. He walked up behind her. "I will give you $100 if you will go to bed with me." Harper jumped up and spun around to face him.

"Excuse me?"

"Don't look so shocked. Jess told me all about you and her father."

"That was a long time ago. I was just a stupid kid then. That is not part of my life I think about."

"Once a whore always a whore."

"Craig you are being really inappropriate right now. Please step out of my way."

"This is my apartment baby. I will do anything I want." He leaned in and kissed her neck. She pulled away.

"Craig you have been drinking."

"Here baby have good taste of what I have been drinking" He kissed her hard on the mouth. She pulled away. She slapped him. "So you want it rough do you?"

"I don't want anything at all. Get away from me." She shoved him. He pushed her in return. She fell against the wall. "Craig please stop." She regained her footing.

"You think you can just come in here and live rent free. And not give me anything in return? Do you?" He grabbed her arm. With her free arm Harper punched

Craig in the nose. "You little bitch." He spoke through clinched teeth as blood trickled from his nose. He grabbed her by the neck and started chocking her. She kicked him in the knee. He doubled over in pain. She ran toward the door. He got ahead of her. He threw himself between her and the door. He threw her to the floor. He was a top her in seconds. She fought with all her might. It was in vain. His strength was overpowering.

He stood and zipped his pants. He threw a ten dollar bill onto the floor next to her. "You better get yourself cleaned up. Jess and Marilyn will be back soon. He crossed the room and walked out the door. Harper lie there on the cold, hard floor. Broken. Hot tears burned her face. From someplace beyond herself she found enough strength to pull herself out of the floor. She left Craig's filthy $10. lying on the floor. She carried her fragile body into the shower. She turned the water on hot and full blast. She peeled off her clothes. She stepped

into the shower. She slid down into the floor. Sitting.

She pulled her knees to her chest. She buried her head

against her knees. The hot water burned her skin. She

did not feel it. She sat there in a fog. The water ran cold.

Harper still sat there. She was only brought back to

reality when there was a knock at the door.

"Mama I need to go pee." Like a robot Harper turned

off the water. She wrapped herself in a towel and walked

past Marilyn, without a word. Harper couldn't look at

Marilyn or anyone. Not yet. She went to her bedroom.

She threw on a baggie t shirt and sweatpants. She

wondered how much more of her could die a little at a

time and technically still be living. She plopped onto the

bed and drifted at least a million miles away. Her mind

took her to a time before mama got herself killed in the

car crash. Harper remember being curled up in mama's

lap safe and sound. They would sometimes sit for hours. Mama would read aloud to Harper. Mama always had a book close at hand. The stories mama read to Harper always made her feel as though anything was possible. After mama died the only thing possible was surviving, typicality she struggled to do that. Harper's thought were interpreted by a knock at the door. Without waiting for an answerer Jess burst into the room.

"We are ordering pizza for supper. My treat. What do you- Harper what's wrong? Did you have a hard day in the laundry?"

"Don't make fun of me Jess."

"I wasn't. I just-"

"Could you watch Marilyn this evening? I am really wiped out. I just want to sleep for a while."

"Harper is something wrong? You know you can tell me anything."

Yeah right Jess. I will just tell you anything. Can I tell you your boyfriend raped me this afternoon while you and Marilyn were having ice cream? "Really Jess I just need some rest."

"Okay. Watching Marilyn is no trouble. We will get plenty of food if you case you change your mind" Jess closed the door and was gone.

Alone in her bedroom Harper wondered how easy it would be to take her life. The thought had crossed her mind before. When she found out she was pregnant, when Bradley died. When Harold and Katherine died. When Less robbed her blind. When she lost her house. She had thought to herself who would care if I am gone? Who would care if I take myself out of this cycle of misery and heartbreak? Who would even care? Who would even notice? She felt fairly confident that Jess would provide for Marilyn. They had bonded overnight.

Jess was successful she could give Marilyn a completely different life. In a way wouldn't Harper be doing Marilyn a favor? Harper sat there in the dark facing this new lowest point with a bottle of sleeping pills in one hand and a beer in the other. She opened the bottle and took a few pills. She chased the pills down with the beer. The pain would end soon. Deep seductive sleep gently pulled her under.

The next morning Marilyn ran into the room. "Mama, Jess and I made breakfast." Marilyn shook Harper's shoulder. Harper was motionless. Marilyn ran to the kitchen. "Jess, mama wouldn't wake up."

"What do you mean you cant wake her up?" Jess was sitting the kitchen table. She sat the plates in her hand down.

"I shook her. She didn't budge."

"Okay I will check on her. She said she was really

tired yesterday." Jess and Marilyn walked into the bedroom. Jess rolled Harper onto her back and checked her pulse.

"Does she have a pulse? Is she okay?"

"Yes sweetheart she has a pulse. Can you go and get Craig?" Jess didn't want to alarm Marilyn, but Harper's pulse was weak and thready. Marilyn returned in seconds with Craig close behind. As Craig entered the room he spotted the beer can and pill bottle.

"There's her problem." As he spoke he reached under the bed and picked up the bottle and can.

"Crap Harper what have you done?"Jess exclaimed as she ran from the room. Craig and Marilyn followed. Jess grabbed the phone and called 911. Harper woke up a bit later. Jess was standing next to her with her arms crossed. "What were you thinking? That stunt would have killed anyone else." Harper slowly woke. She

100

rubbed her eyes and looked around.

"Where am I?"

"In the hospital. You are damn freaking lucky you are not in the morgue. You know Marilyn was the one who found you this morning. Do you know how scared she was? How terrified she was. Really Harper what were you thinking? Honestly I don't know what is so bad that you would try to take your life. You are living rent free. You have a job. You have a daughter who adores you. I don't know why, but she does. And what? You would just throw it all away? You are no better than your father. You know Craig and I have been talking. We would be happy to help you find a place of your own, but Marilyn should stay with us for a while. You can, of course come and visit. A once you get yourself lined out a bit we will see about you getting her back." Harper sat straight up in bed.

"Get her back? She's my daughter Jess. Did you forget that?"

"No Harper don't get upset. This isn't the kind of life an eight year old needs to be living. I mean what the hell Harper?   First Marilyn was in the hospital it because she fell out of a chair she with standing in trying to get you coffee. Now your here because you tried to kill yourself. Remember how much you hated how Charlie raised you? Are you a better parent than him or worse?"

"You know what else an eight year old doesn't need? She doesn't need to live with a rapist. That's what she doesn't need."

"What foolishness are you talking about?"

"Jess why do you think I tried to kill myself? Have you stopped to think about that? Your precious Craig raped me yesterday."

"That's bullshit. And you know it."

"Is it? Apparently someone told him what I once told you about trading sex for money with your father. Craig offered me $100. if I would sleep with him. I refused. We got into a knock down drag out. He raped me and threw ten dollars at me."

"There is not a syllable of truth to that. Harper how could you even think about saying something like that?"

"Jess get this damned iv out of my arm right now or I will pull it out myself."

"Harper you need to stay until your doctor releases you."

"Why? So you can have enough time to plot how to take my child away from me?"

"No we will work something out."

"What is there to work out? You are not taking my child way from me.   She is all I have."

"Okay I am sorry.   I shouldn't have said anything.

What are you in such a hurry to get out of here for?"

"Are you kidding? You don't believe me about Craig and you want to take my child away from me? Am I supposed to just stay here? Seriously Jess are you taking this damned iv out or am I" Against her better judgment Jess removed the iv.

"Where are you going to go?"

"You don't care."

"Harper I do care. I am trying to be a good friend to you."

"A friend? A friend would believe me about Craig. The world has knocked me down so many times how much am I supposed to take? Finding you after all of these years felt like such a blessing. Now when I need you to be my friend the most you don't believe me. So no Jess I am not staying here. Marilyn is sure as hell not staying here. I hope you and Craig have a nice long life together. You deserve each other. You are two of a kind." Harper stormed out of the room. She collected Marilyn from the waiting room and they left the hospital.

"Mama I like it here. Why do we always have to move? I like my school. I have friends. Jess is my sister. We are becoming friends."

"Marilyn the next place will be better."

"That's what you said last time. I want to stay with Jess and Craig. Jess said I could stay."

"That bitch. When did she say that to you?"

"That's not a very nice word."

"Well she is not a very nice person."

"Yes she is. She bakes cookies. She know more about being a mom than you do."

"Oh does she? I bet she told you to say that didn't she?"

"No mama I said it all on my own. If I lived with Craig and Jess I would never have to move or eat food out of the trash."

"Now you listen to me young lady. Jess is not your mother. I am. Until you are eighteen you will do as I say. Now get in the backseat and buckle up. Not another word. Do you understand me?"

"Yes mama." They drove away. Into the sunset. Into the unknown, again.

Chapter 15

There would be no more men. At fifteen Trevor had been a ugly first taste of love. He had used Harper as a punching bag when ever the mood struck him. Less had swooped in and rescued her. She nearly laughed out loud as her mind drifted back to him telling her he would show her what a real man was. And then there was Bradley. Harper's eyes still fluttered with tears whenever she thought about him. Harper knew Bradley would always remain her once in a lifetime. He had been everything all girls dream of. He had bought her flowers, held doors. He had even written her poems. Sure they were crap, but she knew she would treasure them always. He had stepped in and been an amazing father for Marilyn. He had taught her how to ride a bike, how to fish, how to throw a perfect curve ball. The important stuff. The daddy stuff. Marilyn still called him Daddy Bradley. Harper hoped she always would. She hoped that their memories of Bradley would travel with both of them for the rest of their lives. Then there was Craig. Harper recognized that Craig, in away brought the men she had known full circle. Craig and Trevor had both been violent. She also knew that so much of the shit she had experienced with the men in her life had risen from her relationship or lack there of with Charlie. Since she knew she could not, would not go home again. Could not would not come to terms with Charlie, there would be no more men.

Harper and Marilyn landed in a new town. Harper quickly found a job and a small apartment. It felt good to focus n Marilyn. They spent quality time at the park, the roller rink, the shopping mall, and the movies. Harper was reconnecting with her daughter as well as with herself. She had not had as much as an aspirin since the night of her suicide attempt. Harper was amazed at how incredible it felt to be clear headed. It was magnificent to be high on ice cream, cotton candy, the crisp cool spring air and Marilyn. Like had opened itself up to Harper in ways she had never known. Life had begun. New. Fresh. Harper had even enrolled in courses at the community college. She wasn't sure what degree she wanted. She was focused on getting the basics out of the way. She was loving every minute of it.

Marilyn was thriving as well. She had settled into her new school. She had made several friends. Her teacher said that Marilyn was one of the smartest children in he class. Her grades reflected that. She was making straight A's. For the first time in her young life she was talking about her future.

He was her history professor. Harper noticed him the second he walked through the door the first night of class. He wore his hair short. He had a healthy tan. His clothes were exquisite. He wore a slate gray suit with a periwinkle shirt. She wondered how important it was to swear off men? Turned out he had noticed her as well. In the margin of a graded paper he had wrote "call me sometime." She waited for everyone else to leave, then she approached him

"I could report you for this." She aid as she pointed to his number on her paper.

"Yes, but you are not going to." He gave her a sly grin.

"What makes you so sure?"

"I have caught you looking at me a time or two. So are you going to put that number to use or not?"

"Probably not. You are my professor and-"

"Of course there is someone else."

"No there is no one else. I am trying to focus on myself and my daughter right now."

"You have been burned more than your fair share of times so you have decided to swear off relationships."

"Yes exactly."

"Then how do you know whether or not there's a man in front of you who is unlike anything you have ever known?"

"I guess I will just have to risk it." Harper turned and

walked out the door.

Every assignment she turned in came back with a note on it. She read it and then forced him out of her mind. The end of the semester rolled around. One last assignment, one last note. "Give me one chance to prove I am not the others. Meet me Saturday at the movie theater." A movie? What was so special about a movie? She had been taken to hundreds of movies over the years. Still there was something intriguing about the invitation. So, against her better judgment she arrived at the movie theater on Saturday night. When she arrived there was only three cars in the parking lot. That was odd. The place was usually packed, especially on Saturdays. Feeling a little apprehensive Harper parked and walked toward the door. As she reached for the door a young man opened it for her.

"Ms. Harper Miller? Right this way. Mr. Winthrop

is waiting for you." Harper followed the usher into the darkened theater. As they entered Harper noticed that all the seats were empty. All except for one. As Morgan heard the door open and close he turned to face them. He stood in the center of the room. He held a long stem rose in one hand and a box of popcorn in the other. The usher quietly left the room. Harper walked toward Morgan. He handed her the rose.

"I also have nachos, and raisinets. I can go back for anything else you want."

"You bought out the entire theater for us?"

"Yes but there is more." They sat down and the movie came on. Harper recognized it at once.

""Rear Window" How did you know that was one of my favorite movies?"

"I have my sources. We have a few mutual friends."

"I am not sure if that is impressive or creepy. I am

willing to let it go for now."

After the movie Morgan walked Harper to her car. They walked hand in hand. Harper found herself thinking it felt really good to hold his hand. They reached her car. She fished her keys out of her purse and opened the door. "So Morgan just what does one top buying out a movie theater and having them show whatever you want?"

"There is just one way to find out."

"You will call me then?"

"I will call you." He gently kissed her check. He watched her until her car was out of sight. They both felt as though something rather extraordinary had begun. "Good morning. I hope I am not calling to early."

"No not at all." Truth be told the phone had woke her up. She was so glad to hear from him she didn't care how early on a Sunday morning it was.

"Do you have to work today? Or are you free?"

"No. Our day is wide open"

"Good I am glad to hear that. Could you and Marilyn come and meet me around 11am?"

"You want Marilyn to come with us?"

"Yes I would like to get to know you both. If that's okay."

"I'd like that. What do you have planned for us?"

"You will have to wait and see." He gave her an address, she jotted it down. They hung up.

"Where are we going mama?" Marilyn aid as she climbed into the backseat. Harper got in and pulled the car onto the road.

"I don't know Marilyn. Morgan wanted it to be a surprise."

"How well do you know this guy mama? Basically we are going some place with a stranger. You're not supposed to do that."

"Marilyn I know him. It's okay. I think he is a nice guy. I think you will too." About twenty minutes later they arrived at the address Morgan had given. It was a building in a large open field. As they approached the building they saw a sign on the building , "Somewhere Over The Rainbow Hot Air Balloon Adventures."

"Hot air balloon!" Marilyn squealed with excitement.

"See there. Its already better than you thought it was going to be." Marilyn didn't hear what her mother had said. She had already darted from the car. Morgan pulled up next to them. He walked over to them.

"Marilyn this is Mr. Winthrop."

"You can just call me Morgan."

"Are we really going hot air ballooning?"

"Marilyn take a minute and say hello."

"Hello. Are we really going hot air ballooning?"

"I take it I made a good call?"

"Oh yes Marilyn has always wanted to ride in an hot air balloon."

"And you?"

"I'm game. I will try anything once." The floated peacefully around the city. Marilyn was completely mesmerized. She couldn't stop staring wide eyed at the seenry below. "Look mama, there's my school. Look mama I think that our apartment. Look mama there is the store." Morgan noticed Harper was feeling a little queasy. He put his arms around her. They cut the trip short and landed.

"I hope you will like what else I have planned a bit more." Morgan said as he got out of the balloon. He helped both Harper and Marilyn done. "Right this way ladies." They followed him to a red gingham table cloth. On it was a wicker picnic basket. "I didn't know what either of you would like so I've brought an assortment."

They sat down. Morgan unpacked the basket. He brought fried chicken, potato salad, deli sandwiches, cheese cake, and apple cider. The three of them sat there in the beautiful afternoon sun. They laughed and talked the day away. Harper opened up to Morgan about all of the demons of the past. Morgan and Marilyn hit it off instantly. Harper loved how good he was with Marilyn. These was the first of many days the three of them would spend together.

Harper found it odd that Morgan never spoke of his life or brought up plans for their future. She tried not to dwell on it though. She knew she was falling passionately crazy in love with him. He rented them a small house, but he would never stay. They went to bed together. She always woke up alone. There would always be a note on his pillow, an excuse. He just had to leave. She forced herself to believe his excuses. In the back of her mind she knew the truth. They lie naked in each others arms. "Are you married Morgan? Please be honest with me." Long empty silence stretched out between them. "Morgan please say something."

"Harper I love you. I love you not her." Harper got up out of bed and crossed the room to the window. She stared out into the vast darkness. He walked up behind her. He placed his hands on her shoulders and kissed her neck. She abruptly spun around to face him.

"Don't touch me."

"Harper please. She doesn't make me happy anymore. I want to be here with you and Marilyn. Think of how happy we have been together. Think of how happy we can continue to be. Me being married doesn't change how much I love you and Marilyn. Nothing has to change. Have you suddenly stopped loving me?"

"You can't expect me to live as the other woman."

"Of course not. I will leave her, just give me a little time. In the mean time I have something for you." He picked his pants up off the floor and took a small box out of the pocket. "Open it." She took it from him and opened it. It was a sterling silver heart on a chain. In the center of the heart there were three birthstones: Harper's, Morgan's and Marilyn's. "You and Marilyn are my heart. Will you wear it?" Harper nodded yes. Morgan placed the chain around her neck. The silver heart glistened in the moonlight as it fell against Harper's bare skin. He pulled her into his arms. He kissed her. Her body ached for his. She craved him more than air or nourishment. A million times stronger than her ache for his body was the crippling ache in her very soul. It screamed at her telling her that she would never leave him. She knew that living with the pain of being the other woman would hurt less than the pain of living without him.

They soon fell into a comfortable routine. Morgan spent as much time with Harper and Marilyn as he could. Harper mentioned Morgan leaving his wife from time to time. She didn't want to bring up the subject too often, she was scared to death if she did she would scare him away for good. When she did ask his answer was always the same "I need just a bit more time. Don't give up on us. Trust me I need just a bit more." Time passed as time usually does. Soon it had been a year since Morgan confessed to Harper that he was married. Harper knew that they could no longer go on like this. Yet she couldn't bring herself to break it off.

As far as Harper was concerned there was one more option she would do for Morgan the one thing she knew his wife had never done. She would give him a child. Her plan worked quickly. A baby was soon on the way.

Harper lie awake at night unable to sleep. She couldn't stop daydreaming about how she was going to tell Morgan about the baby. Suddenly he interrupted her thoughts "My wife is dying." Harper rolled over to face him, locking her eyes to his.

"What do you mean she is dying."

"Just that. She is dying. She has been having headaches for a while now. I finally talked her into going to have it checked out. They found a brain tumor. Her doctor says she has a few months left. Obviously I can't leave her. And I can't openly be with anyone else for an appropriate amount of time after she is gone. So-"

"You are breaking up with me?"

"No. No I'm only saying we need to take a break. This house is yours Harper. You and Marilyn can stay here as long as you like. When the appropriate time comes we will see where we stand." Harper turned away from him as hot tears burned her face. Without thinking words poured from her mouth. "I am pregnant. Morgan if you leave me you will be leaving your child. Can you leave your child?" They lie there in painful silence for what seemed like forever. At first Harper wasn't sure Morgan had heard her or not, but she didn't dare repeat what she had said. At last he spoke.

"I have to be there for her now Harper."

"So that's just it then? You want nothing to do with this child?"

"I didn't say that. We don't have to figure anything out right now."

"That's always your answer isn't it? Always putting things off until some later time. I think you need to go. Go home an sit and watch your wife die. But don't expect me and Marilyn and your baby to be sitting here waiting for you when you get back." Harper retrieved

Morgan's t-shirt from the floor, slipped it over her head and walked from the bedroom. He quickly pulled on his pants and followed her. They sat opposite each other at the kitchen table. Morgan reached out and cupped her hands in his. "Harper I don't want to loose you. Please give me some more time. I promise you a soon as the time is right we will be married. You, Marilyn, our baby, and I will be a family." Harper noticed a stray tear trickle away from Morgan's eyes. Harper leaned in and kissed him with a haunting sweetness. They both stood. Harper took Morgan's hand and led him to the bedroom. Their bodies were one in an instant. Harper knew she would not, could not live without Morgan. There would be no life.

It was a cold, rainy October morning. Blinding labor pains woke Harper. She called Morgan's number there was no answer. She tried again and again there was no answer. The baby was coming a lot faster than Marilyn had. After calling Morgan's number no less than ten times she knew she had no chose but to call the ambulance. Three hours and twenty minutes later Grace Kelly Winthrop arrived. Across town at the very same moment Morgan's wife took her last breath. As her final breath escaped from her lungs her hand went cold and limp, slipping from Morgan's. Like a child he ran from the house. He kept running. They had never loved one another. Not the way you are supposed to love the person you commit to for better or worse. They had been compatible. They liked the same art, the same books. They had met at a time in their lives when they were both tired of trying to find love. Who has time for it anyway? Career had been more important to them both. What brought them together was that they had both been sick of attending functions alone. Sad, yes but true. Morgan burst though the door of Harper's house. The house was empty. Morgan found a note on the kitchen table. "Mama is having the baby. We are at the hospital."

Morgan walked into Harper's hospital room. The sight before his eye melted his heart. Harper was holding their baby, Marilyn was curled up next to her. Harper felt him walk into the room. She looked up at him. "Come and meet your daughter." Morgan crossed the room in long strides. He at down next to the bed. Harper placed their baby in his arms. "I named her Grace, I hope hat is okay." Morgan held his daughter close and nodded. Harper could see sadness in Morgan's eyes. "Morgan what's wrong?"

"She's gone. She died a few hours ago," Harper gathered him into her arms. They cried as one.

Morgan moved in with Harper the day after his wife's funeral. People talked. People are going to talk no matter what you do. They were a family. Harper knew it in her very core. She knew this was it. Life had finally settled into what she knew it should be. Morgan proposed right away, they were married within three months. They moved out of the small house in the city to a spacious farm house in the country. They even got a dog. They settled into a life that felt like a dream. The funny thing about something being too good to be true is, it almost always is.

Harper's gut knew something was wrong from the beginning Her heart refused to listen. The phone would ring, Harper would answer and there would be no none on the other end. Morgan had always come home from work late, but late kept getting later and later. There were nights when he didn't come home at all. One afternoon

Harper came home early. She went into house. Marilyn

at on the couch wrapped up in a book. She had

headphones on. Two year Grace sat in front of the

television lost in a brightly colored cartoon. "Where is

Morgan?"

"One of his students stopped by. He said they needed

somewhere to study. They are upstairs, in your bedroom.

Harper turned and rushed upstairs. She kept telling

herself she couldn't be right. Slowly she opened the

door. Harper felt as though someone had kicked her in

the stomach. She felt as though her very last breath had

been violently knocked from her body. She trembled

from head to toe. In her bed before her very eyes her

husband and a girl who looked barely legal were having

sex. In her bed. Neither of them noticed Harper. She

walked out the door and across the hall to the bathroom.

Harper washed her face and took a deep breath. Harper

took a bright red lipstick out of the medicine cabinet.

With shaking hands she wrote on the mirror. "Once your

little study session is over, pack a bag. Do not be here

when I get back." Harper took several more deep

breaths and went downstairs. "Guys lets go get a pizza."

She stepped in front of the tv and turned it off. They left

the house.

Chapter 16

Their waiter was about 19 years old. Harper noticed

his blue eyes were very warm and kind. Something about

him sparked something within her very soul. He openly

flirted with Harper throughout the evening. She

reminded herself that wait staff routinely flirt with

customers. Besides she was married and he was much

closer to Marilyn's age than to Harper's. Still, at the end

of the evening when he wrote his name and number on

the receipt Harper didn't throw it away. She put it safe

and sound in her billfold. She found herself wanting to see him again.

When they returned home Morgan was sitting at the kitchen table. "Marilyn would you please take your sister upstairs and help her get ready for bed. Your mother and I need to talk." Marilyn and Grace went upstairs.

"There is nothing to talk about. I asked you to leave."

"You know you don't want me to leave." Morgan took Harper's arm and pulled her in close. She pulled away.

"You can't be serious right now. You can't expect me to forgive you? I walked in on you and a girl in our bed. While my children were just feet away? That's sick Morgan. Sick."

"It won't happen again."

"No? Which part of it? With the kids in the house? With a student? In our bed? Getting caught?"

"None of it. I will never cheat on you again Harper. Please Harper." He passionately pulled her into his arms. "Please give me a second chance. Please give us a second chance." He brushed a stray strand of hair away from her face and kissed her neck. Harper fought the urge to stay in his arms and forgive him instantly. Her mind raced back to when she had been some girl in his wife's bed. Harper knew she couldn't flip the switch on how crazy in love with him she was. She knew it would break Marilyn and Grace's hearts if she pulled them away from him.

"I can't forgive you tonight or tomorrow. Maybe not ever. I also know I cant stop loving you tonight or tomorrow. Maybe not ever. That's why this hurts so bad." They were both in tears. Morgan gathered her into his arms.

"I know. We can do is Harper. One second. One

minute. One day."

The next day Harper ran into the sexy young waiter from the night before. A conversation quickly struck up between them. They made plans to meet for coffee the next day. They met for coffee everyday that week. Their friendship felt really good. At first Harper thought the eleven years between the would be an issue. It wasn't. "Reggie that is a name you don't hear that often. I bet there is a story behind it?"

"Really? Somebody named Harper is going to ask me about my name? But yeah you're right, There is a story. My mom is a big time Elton John fan. She wanted to name me Elton. Dad wouldn't hear of it. So mom named me Reginald. It never occurred to dad that Reginald is Elton's given name. And yourself?"

"I guess our moms thought alike in a way. My mom

wanted to be a writer. Her favorite book was "To Kill A Mockingbird." So she named me Harper Lee."

"Did your mom ever become a writer. Do I know anything she has written?"

"She never got the chance. She died in a car crash years ago."

"What about your dad?"

"I don't know. I can't deal with Charlie, my dad. Shit happened that it hurts to even think about because of him. I left when I was pregnant with Marilyn. I won't ever go back."

"I am sorry." Reggie reached across the table and took her hand in his. A dark cloud had descended upon her, he wanted so badly to deliver her from it. "Hey do you have some time? Will you go for a drive with me? Wait here. Give me ten minutes I will be right back." Without waiting for Harper to answer Reggie got up and practically ran from the coffee house. True to his word he was back in under ten minutes. They drove for twenty minutes. They were well out of town.

"You're not going to murder me are you?"

"If I were would I tell you? We are going slow enough that you could totally jump out and survive. I know we are out of the way, trust me it is worth it." As he spoke he pulled into a private drive. "This place belongs to my grandparents." He pulled alongside a lake in the middle of a large field.

"Your grandparents own this? It looks for like a park."

"Yeah. Its land that has been in the family for several generations. I come here when I need a place to think" He got out of the truck and came around to open her door. He took a picnic basket and blanket out of the back. They spreed out the blanket and sat down.

"You know Charlie's place had a lake."

"I'm sorry. Do you want to go somewhere else?"

"No. Its perfect here. You had no way of knowing that. You know I haven't thought about him in years here lately he has been on my mind a lot."

"Maybe it would be helpful to get all of it out. Why did you run away?"

"Marilyn's dad was Charlie's best friend. At first I thought being with him was so cool. He bought me things I was an easily impressed child. I turned up pregnant. I was scared, of course. I told Charlie about the relationship. He didn't believe me. He choose his scum friend over his own daughter." Uncontrollable tears poured forward. Reggie took Harper into his arms. Emotions and clouded judgment took over them. They made love as the warm sun washed over them.

Reggie and Harper quickly fell into a routine. They

met at his grandparents lake nearly everyday. Neither one of them could get enough. Being together was like a drug, or a spell they had fallen under. Harper craved him. The more she was with him the more she wanted, needed hm. Harper soon discovered that she was pregnant. She was so excited to share the news with Reggie. They lie naked on the blanket. Harper rolled over on her side and gentle caressed his face. "I am pregnant." Reggie bolted up, off the ground and into his pants.

"What? No you're playing a sick joke." Harper quickly dressed and stood next to him.

"You're not happy?"

"No Harper I am not happy. Maybe its Morgan's."

"I don't understand why you are upset."

"Harper I am nineteen years old. I am leaving for college in the fall. Am I supposed to give up my dreams to raise this child? This child is Morgan's. As far as I am concerned this child is Morgan's. I can go with you to the abortion clinic for support or whatever but that is it." Less's words from a dozen years ago came back and slapped Harper upside the head. Harper began briskly walking to her car. "Harper where are you going?"

"Have a nice life Reg. Good luck with college. And all the important stuff you are going to be doing." He didn't try to stop her. She didn't look back.

Chapter 17

Marilyn had began to blossom into a beautiful young woman. She stood at the kitchen sink. Her back was turned to Morgan. He could tell she was crying. Morgan walked up behind Marilyn and wrapped his arms around her waist. She fought free. "Morgan!"

"Come on baby. Let daddy Morgan make it all better." He grabbed her again. Marilyn fought with everything she had. Morgan was stronger. He kissed her.

She bit, kicked, and hit him. The more she fought the more aggressive he became. Then as suddenly as it had began it was over. Morgan lie unconscious at Marilyn's feet. Harper stood over him, a cast iron frying pan in her hand. Blood oozed from Morgan's head.

"Get your sister and run to the car. I will be right there."

"Mama!"

"Get you sister and go to the car. Go Marilyn. Go." Marilyn scooped up Grace and ran from the house. Harper was seconds behind them. They piled into the car and drove off in a cloud of dust. "Marilyn are you alright? Did he hurt you? Do you understand what I am asking you?"

"Yes mama I understand. No he didn't hurt me."

"Has anything like that happened before?"

"No mama. Is he dead?"

"I don't know."

"You didn't check?"

"Lets not worry about that Marilyn okay? You're safe. Grace is safe. Lets just put some distance between ourselves and Morgan." The men in Harper's life had been shitty to her more than she carried to admit. But her children had never been harmed until now. The thought of what had nearly happened between Morgan and Marilyn made Harper ill. No man in Harper's life would ever harm her children again. And to that end, she knew there was only one place left to go. To go forward she now knew there was no choose but to go back.

Chapter 18

He sat on the porch playing guitar. As the car pulled into the driveway he sat his guitar down and walked toward the car. Harper got out of the car and walked toward him. They met each other halfway. Neither one spoke. They enveloped each other in a hug. Harper spilled tears on Charlie's shoulder as he did hers. "You've come home."

"Oh Charlie we had no where else left to go." Harper motioned for Marilyn and Grace to get out of the car. They did and stood next to their mother. "These are my girls, Grace and Marilyn. Would it be alright for us to stay for a few days?"

"Stay as long as you like."

"We drove all night. The girls are beat."

"Let's go inside. They can nap in your old bedroom." Harper settled Marilyn and Grace into her childhood bedroom and joined Charlie at the kitchen table. "What brings you here?"

"Life. Every decision I have ever made has led me back to this kitchen table." Harper gave Charlie the condensed version of what had happened since she left thirteen years earlier. "Morgan, my husband, I thought he was different. Turned out he was different all right. I walked into our kitchen the other day to find him groping Marilyn. Charlie I hit him over the head with a cast iron skillet."

"Is he dead?"

"No. He wasn't when we left him."

"I should have stood up for you that way when you told me about Less. Instead I called you a liar. I couldn't force myself to believe that someone who had been like a brother to me could have betrayed me that way."

"Sometimes the people who are supposed to love us the most are the ones who hurt us the most."

"I resented you when you were a child. After your mom died I couldn't get it out of my head that it was your fault. If she hadn't drove off that night trying to get the

140

two of you away from me. Every time I looked at you all

I could think was "If it wasn't for this snotty faced little

brat my Charlotte would still be alive." Just then

Marilyn appeared in the doorway.

"Mama, Grace is having trouble getting to sleep."

Harper got up from the table.

"I am going to take care of my children now." She left

Charlie sitting at the kitchen table. Coming home had

been such a mistake. They would have to leave again in

the morning. Harper would not stay in a house with

someone so hateful. Sometime during the night Harper

was jolted out of a sound sleep. She heard someone in

the bathroom throwing up.   Harper jumped up from the

floor where she had been sleeping. Both girls were still

in the bed sound asleep. Harper knew it had to be

Charlie. Harper went to him. She found him on his

hands and knees in front of the toilet. His shirt was

covered with blood. "Good God Charlie. What did you do? Snort too much heroin or something?"

"I haven't done any of that in years."

"Then what the hell happened?"

"Its nothing. Don't worry about it." Charlie stood and started for the door. Harper noticed he was unsteady she took his arm. She led him to the kitchen table. He sat down. Harper got Charlie a glass of water. She sat down.

"You are sick aren't you? What is it?"

"Lung cancer. I don't have long."

"Before you said you are not using drugs anymore. How long?"

"After you ran away."

"Why not before? Why not before mama left you that last time? All she wanted was for us to be a family. All she ever wanted was for you to get clean and sober. You couldn't give her that one thing. One thing." Harper was in tears now. "My fault she's gone? No sir. That is all you. Charlie I grew up without a parent. Do you know what that feels like?"

"I know more than you realize. My brother and I grew up with a mean alcoholic daddy, who beat us for looking at him wrong. Mama was so depressed she never bothered getting out of bed. She ended up killing herself after your Uncle Corey died. Mama blamed me for Corey being gone. Daddy blamed me for mama killing herself. Now here you are blaming me for everything? Harper Lee Miller if you need someone to blame, you find yourself a mirror." Charlie stormed out of the room. Harper heard him slam his bedroom door.

Harper sat at the kitchen table for the rest of the night. Her life played like a movie in her mind. By morning Harper knew Charlie was right. All the years of hating him lifted from her. The whole cabin felt lighter. As though a dark cloud had drifted past, away for good. Both girls were still asleep. Harper went to check on Charlie.

"Harper would you come and sit with me for awhile?" Harper sat down on the edge of Charlie's bed. His face held no color. His energy was zapped. "Your mother's journal is in the top dresser drawer." Charlie struggled to force his words to come. His breath was shallow and labored. "I want you to have it. I robbed you of knowing her. The least I can do is give you her journal, give you a sense of who she was." Harper took Charlie into her arms. They cried together. Suddenly she felt his body go limp. His last breath hit her in the face and vanished. He was gone. Harper gently lowered Charlie onto his pillow.

Chapter 19

Charlie's funeral was two days later. Harper and the children were the only ones there. No one else showed up. It was a simple graveside service at a cemetery a few miles away from Charlie's farm. The preacher came over to introduce himself. "Hello. I am Reverend Dirk Lightfoot. Should we wait for your husband? Or do you want to get started?"

"My husband?"

"I assumed. You are expecting aren't you?"

"Oh yes. No, my husband is-" Dead? Out of the picture? "We are separated."

"So this is everyone then?"

"It appears so." After the service Dirk came back over to Harper.

"Would you and your children care to join me for dinner?"

"Oh I don't know."

"You have to eat don't you? There is this great little place in town." They joined Dirk for dinner. The four of

145

them hit it off beautifully. It felt as though Dirk had always been in their lives. They saw more and more of him. Soon Harper and Dirk were very much in love. Dirk didn't flinch when Harper told him about Morgan. In fact Dirk help her face it. As it turned out Morgan was fine. He agreed not to press charges, as long as she agreed to work with him on shared custody of Grace. Morgan also agreed to a divorce.

Harper and Reggie's baby was born. Harper named the baby Elton. Harper and Dirk were married a year to the day after they met. Dirk immediately started the process of adopting all three children. Harper sold Charlie's farm and the cabin. She and Dirk bought a house in town. The past was gone and Harper knew it. There would be no more running. Five miles away from where she had spent her childhood, Harper knew she was home. Never in her wildest dreams had she ever imagined she would be a preachers wife but she couldn't

imagine her life any other way.

Made in the USA
Charleston, SC
26 May 2015